This edition published by Parragon Books Ltd in 2017 and distributed by

Parragon Inc.
440 Park Avenue South, 13th Floor
New York, NY 10016
www.parragon.com

ISBN 978-1-4748-8316-0

Printed in China

Disney

Aladdin

MAGICAL STORY
COLLECTION

Bath · New York · Cologne · Melbourne · Delhi
Hong Kong · Shenzhen · Singapore

Deep in the Arabian Desert, there was an evil sorcerer, Jafar. He had paid a thief called Gazeen to steal a golden scarab beetle for him.

Jafar held the beetle up and watched it glow with magic.

The golden creature flew into the warm desert air.
"Come on, Gazeen!" Jafar cried.
They followed the magic beetle as it led them toward
the Cave of Wonders.

Jafar ordered Gazeen to enter the cave.
A huge tiger leapt out.

"Only one may enter here . . ." growled
the tiger ". . . the Diamond in the Rough!"

The entrance to the cave collapsed
and Gazeen was buried alive!

Jafar crept away. "I must find this
Diamond in the Rough," he whispered.

The next morning, the marketplace in Agrabah was full of people.

An orphan boy called Aladdin stared hard at a loaf of bread. His tummy rumbled. He reached out. . . .

"Stop, thief!" shouted the Sultan's head palace guard, and Aladdin raced away.

Aladdin made his way back to his simple rooftop home.
He sat with his pet monkey, Abu, and gazed at the palace.

"Some day, we'll have money," he said,
"and we'll never have any problems again."

But in the palace, someone did have problems.

In three days' time, Princess Jasmine was about to
marry a prince she'd never met.

"I want to marry for love," the princess told her
father. "Maybe I don't want to be a princess any more."

The Sultan thought about what Princess Jasmine had said. He loved his daughter. As he tried to come up with a plan, a shadow loomed over him. It was Jafar.

"Ah, my trusted advisor," the Sultan said. "What can I do about Jasmine?"

"Don't worry. Everything will be fine. . . ." said Jafar, holding out his snake staff.

The staff's glowing red eyes cast a spell over the Sultan. In a trance, he handed over his ring that held the mystical blue diamond.

Now, Jafar could use the magic of the ring to find the Diamond in the Rough.

As Jafar made plans,
Princess Jasmine was making
her own plans—to escape.

She stood by the palace walls, with her
faithful tiger.

"I'm sorry, Rajah," she told her giant pet.
"I can't stay here and be forced to marry.
I'll miss you."

She scrambled up the wall and was gone.

Jasmine wandered into the market
and found a small boy. Smiling, she grabbed
an apple from the fruit stall and gave it to him.
She didn't realize she was meant to pay for it!

"Thief!" cried the stall holder.

Aladdin turned up just in time to help.

"She's just confused," he said, and pulled
Jasmine away.

As Jasmine and Aladdin escaped the market, Jafar was in his secret chamber.

He held up the Sultan's ring. "Reveal the Diamond in the Rough!" he commanded.

The ring brought to life a picture of . . . Aladdin!

Meanwhile, Aladdin had taken Jasmine to his home on the roof. In the distance, she could see the palace.

"Where are you from?" Aladdin asked.

"It doesn't matter," she said, turning away from her old home.

There was a sudden clatter on the stairs. Heavy footsteps! Guards burst onto the roof.

Together, Aladdin and Jasmine raced to escape but the guards caught Aladdin.

Jasmine threw off her scarf. "Unhand him," she said, "by order of the princess!"

The captain of the guards narrowed his eyes. "My orders come from Jafar," he said.

Aladdin was thrown into a cell. He'd never see Jasmine again.
An old man sharing his cell heard Aladdin's unhappy story.

"Do something for me and I'll make you rich," the old man said.
He opened up a secret passage.

If money meant
Aladdin could see Jasmine
again, he'd do whatever
his companion wanted!

The old man led Aladdin and Abu into the desert to the Cave of Wonders. He wanted them to find a lamp for him.

The tiger-head entrance recognized Aladdin as the Diamond in the Rough.

"Proceed," the tiger thundered. "Touch nothing but the lamp."

Aladdin found a chamber full of gold. There was a magic carpet, too!

"Can you help us find a lamp?" Aladdin asked the carpet.

The carpet led Aladdin and Abu to a lake deep in the cave. In the center of the lake was the lamp. Aladdin made his way to it, but there was a screech behind him.

His pet monkey had found a glowing gem. He had to have it! "No, Abu!" Aladdin cried, but it was too late.

"You have touched the forbidden treasure!" the tiger said.

Aladdin and Abu raced toward the cave entrance. They were nearly safe when . . . Aladdin fell.

The old man reached out a hand.

"Give me the lamp!"

Aladdin handed it over, but the old man left him to plunge to his death.

The lamp suddenly disappeared from the old man's grasp!
He howled in rage. Ripping off his beard, he revealed that he
was Jafar in disguise.

Aladdin landed safely, thanks to the magic carpet—
and he had the lamp in his hands.

He rubbed it, and a Genie appeared. He could give Aladdin
three wishes, but first he transported them out of the cave.
They were free!

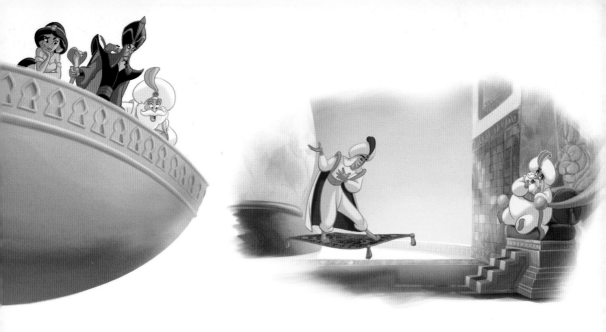

Aladdin made his first wish. "Make me a prince!" he said.

He found himself wearing a prince's clothes and riding in a parade. The parade took him to the palace.

Calling himself Prince Ali Ababwa, Aladdin asked Jasmine to marry him.

"I'm not a prize to be won!" she said, and stormed away.

Aladdin went to her room that night,
still pretending to be Prince Ali Ababwa.

Jasmine glimpsed Aladdin's magic carpet.
She couldn't resist going for a ride!

"You're the boy from the market,"
Jasmine said. He was the prince for her.

Things were going right for Aladdin, finally!

But Jafar tried hard to stop Aladdin and Jasmine from getting married.

His parrot stole the lamp and Jafar made a wish.

"I wish to rule as High Sultan!" he said.

The Genie had no choice but to grant his wish.

Jafar trapped Jasmine in a giant hourglass and hid Aladdin behind a wall of swords.

"The Genie has more power than you'll ever have," Aladdin called, teasing the evil sorcerer. Immediately, Jafar used his final wish. He wanted to become a powerful genie.

He forgot that genies have to obey the master who owns the lamp. . . .

Aladdin held up the lamp and Jafar was sucked down into it. He was going to be held there for all time.

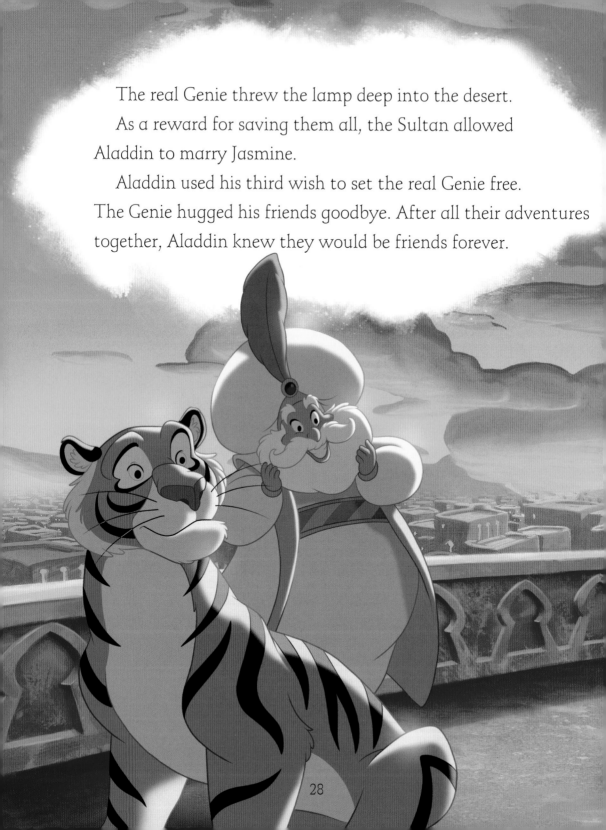

The real Genie threw the lamp deep into the desert.

As a reward for saving them all, the Sultan allowed Aladdin to marry Jasmine.

Aladdin used his third wish to set the real Genie free. The Genie hugged his friends goodbye. After all their adventures together, Aladdin knew they would be friends forever.